I LOVE MY FANGS!

KELLY LEIGH MILLER

**SIMON & SCHUSTER BOOKS
FOR YOUNG READERS**
**New York   London   Toronto
Sydney   New Delhi**

TO MY FAMILY, ALEXANDER, AND THAO

SIMON & SCHUSTER BOOKS FOR YOUNG READERS
An imprint of Simon & Schuster Children's Publishing Division
1230 Avenue of the Americas, New York, New York 10020
Copyright © 2020 by Kelly Leigh Miller
All rights reserved, including the right of reproduction in whole or in part in any form.
SIMON & SCHUSTER BOOKS FOR YOUNG READERS is a trademark of Simon & Schuster, Inc.
For information about special discounts for bulk purchases, please contact
Simon & Schuster Special Sales at 1-866-506-1949 or business@simonandschuster.com.
The Simon & Schuster Speakers Bureau can bring authors to your live event. For more information
or to book an event, contact the Simon & Schuster Speakers Bureau at 1-866-248-3049 or visit our
website at www.simonspeakers.com.
Book design by Lucy Ruth Cummins
The text for this book was hand-lettered.
The illustrations for this book were rendered digitally.
Manufactured in China
0420 SCP
First Edition
2 4 6 8 10 9 7 5 3 1
Library of Congress Cataloging-in-Publication Data
Names: Miller, Kelly Leigh, author, illustrator.
Title: I love my fangs! / Kelly Leigh Miller.
Description: First edition. | New York : Simon & Schuster Books for Young Readers, [2020] |
Audience: Ages 4–8. | Audience: Grades K–1. | Summary: Young Dracula loves his fangs and is very
upset after one falls out—especially when the Tooth Fairy tries to take it away.
Identifiers: LCCN 2019029359 (print) | LCCN 2019029360 (eBook) |
ISBN 9781534452107 (hardcover) | ISBN 9781534452114 (eBook)
Subjects: CYAC: Teeth—Fiction. | Vampires—Fiction.
Classification: LCC PZ7.1.M5815 Iaq 2020 (print) | LCC PZ7.1.M5815 (eBook) | DDC [E]—dc23
LC record available at https://lccn.loc.gov/2019029359
LC eBook record available at https://lccn.loc.gov/2019029360

I LOVE MY FANGS!
THEY ARE POINTY.
THEY ARE SHARP.

THEY ARE A FAMILY TRAIT!

GOOD CARE IS IMPORTANT.

MY FANGS ARE VERY SPECIAL.

POP!

OH NO!!

A VAMPIRE CAN'T HAVE ONLY ONE FANG!

WHAT IF I TAPE IT?

TIE IT?

NO ONE COULD POSSIBLY NOTICE.....

I'M NEVER COMING OUT AGAIN.

ONE FANG IS BETTER THAN NONE.

LOOK AT MY NEW FANG!

AND I CAN'T WAIT FOR
THE OTHER ONE TO POP OUT!